AF069599

Animal Sounds

Written by
Stephen Rickard

2

Animal Sounds

This book without words supports Phase 1 of the phonics programme *Letters and Sounds*. It is also in *Lilac* band, following book bands for guided reading.

About this book

Animal Sounds shows a variety of different animals that should all be known to the children. These animals are all notable for the vocal sounds that they make. The book offers lots of opportunities to extend children's vocabulary as well as their understanding of the world around them.

The animals shown are:
- front cover: a rooster (children may know it as a cockerel)
- page 2: lion, frog
- page 3: a wolf
- page 4: sea lions
- page 5: elephant, bird (a blackbird)
- page 6: howler monkey, humpback whale
- page 7: kitten
- page 8: dog, rooster (or cockerel)

Talk about the book

Read the book with the children, talking about each photograph as you look at it.
- Do the children know what each animal is? Can they name it?
- What do they know about the animal? How big is it? What does it eat? Where does it live?
- How does the animal move? Is it scary, or cute? Friendly or fierce?
- Finally, ask the children what sounds the animal makes. How does it sound when it is sleepy, or hungry, angry, etc.?
- Can they imitate the animal's sounds?

Ransom Reading Stars titles for Letters and Sounds Phase 1 (Phonics) and for Lilac Band

City Sounds	Superhero Salma	**Animal Sounds**
The Ants and the Grasshopper	What are they Playing?	What Can You Hear?
I am a Grown-Up	Time for Bed!	Tell the Robots
The Bus	Animal Homes	Rhyming Pairs
At the Seaside	The Gigantic Turnip	Sound Starters
Hide-and-Seek	At the Skate Park	Tell More Robots
What Rhymes with ... ?	Festivals	Spot the Sounds
The Lost Ball	What Time of Day Is It?	Count the Phonemes
Stripes	The Storm	Odd One Out

Animal Sounds

**Letters and Sounds Phase 1
Lilac book band**
These books have no words

This book links to Aspects 1 and 6 of *Letters and Sounds Phase 1* – General sound discrimination, environmental sounds and Voice sounds.

In particular it supports the following strands:
- Tuning into sounds (auditory discrimination)
- Talking about sounds (developing vocabulary and language comprehension)

More books at this level

 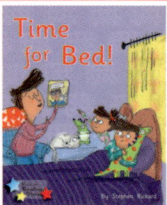   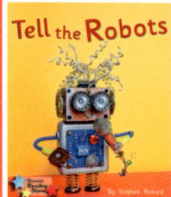

ISBN: 978-1-80047-302-7

www.ransom.co.uk

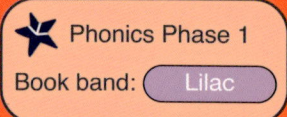
Phonics Phase 1
Book band: Lilac